T3741g

GHOST HORSE
OF THE
PALISADES

By the Same Author

Brother of the Wolves
Don't Forget Michael

GHOST HORSE
OF THE
PALISADES
JEAN THOMPSON

ILLUSTRATED BY
STEPHEN MARCHESI

William Morrow and Company, Inc. / New York

Library of Congress Cataloging in Publication Data
Thompson, Jean, 1933-
Ghost horse of the Palisades.
Summary: Eleven-year-old Molly's quiet life on
the ranch with her widowered father is enlivened by
the reappearance of a mysterious white stallion no
one has ever been able to capture.
[1. Wild horses—Fiction. 2. Horses—Fiction.
3. Ranch life—Fiction] I. Marchesi, Stephen, ill.
II. Title.
PZ7.T371595Gh   1986   [Fic]   85-28496
ISBN 0-688-06145-1

GHOST HORSE
OF THE
PALISADES

Prologue

Night, dark and hushed, covers the lonesome land. There is no moon, but the air is clear and the stars, like ten thousand particles of mica, sparkle in the distant sky. A little wind wanders across the countryside. Now and then it picks up a fallen leaf and turns it over. It gently shakes a bush, setting the living leaves to trembling. The wind blows a little harder and rattles a dead limb so that it groans and rubs against another. Like a tiny echo, some small, quick creature rustles briefly through the foliage and follows the wind into the distance.

There is one light, small and golden, bravely glowing against all the shadows. It is a campfire. Several people gather around it, warming themselves by its light and cheer as much as by its heat.

Their voices murmur softly, reluctant to disturb the vast darkness that gathers around them. They tell each other stories, of comical adventures and brave deeds, of men and women long dead or gone away. They speak of the old times, of winter storms and summer droughts, of cattle trailed and horses bought and sold, of faithful dogs that died. They mention ghosts and apparitions—or at least, some experience with things that no one can quite explain.

Someone tells a story about an old miner who hunted forty fruitless years for a big strike. At last, when he was an old man, he came into town with a pouch full of huge gold nuggets. He bought supplies, mounted his mule and vanished into the wilderness again. Several more times, he came back with his treasure. Unscrupulous men tried to follow him, to find the secret location of his mine and take it for themselves. But the old man was wary and wise. He managed to elude them and cover his trail. Once more the miner came to town, but this time he was very ill. He died without giving away the location of his diggings. Now, somewhere out in the wilds, waiting to be discovered again with all its fantastic golden riches, is the old man's lost mine.

Another person by the campfire tells a tale of the skookum mikter, the big cat, a cougar nearly as tall as a man, who prowls through the thick woods of the Pacific northwest. One time a group of men went into the mountains to hunt it. As they huddled around their campfire at night, a strange wind blew through the trees. Unlike most winds, it didn't blow in a straight line but made a complete circle, rustling invisibly in the shadows beyond the firelight. The horses stampeded, scattering in all directions. Most of the men followed close behind. The skookum mikter was never found and perhaps is still there, far back in the old forests where men never go.

Breaking the silence that follows, a man speaks of a magnificent wild white stallion. He'd chased him once when he was little more than a boy, he says. The pursuit lasted for seven days and nights, but like a phantom, the white horse ran always just beyond their reach. The other horses, the ones ridden by men, pulled up lame, exhausted, and wind-broken, while the wild one galloped on. The men turned back, defeated, and began the slow, painful journey home. They saw the stallion on a ridge above them. His long pale mane and tail tangled in the wind as, head high, untouched, he watched them go.

There never was another horse like the wild white stallion. . . .

/ ONE /

Molly put a final swirl in the frosting and stepped back to admire the cake. The way she'd shaped the thick fudge frosting into scallops and wavy lines made it look almost like a picture in a magazine. A person could hardly tell that the top layer had risen a little bit uneven and sloped to one side.

She carried the cake into the dining room and put it on the hutch. She'd already arranged red and white tulips in the gray pottery bowl. She'd set the table with the good dishes and Mother's wedding silver. She picked a piece of lint off the braided rag rug that her grandmother had made and went back to the kitchen to stir the beef stew.

Oh, if only everything turns out the way I want tonight.

Through the window, she saw Dad was still with Mr. Claypool and his twenty-four-year-old son, Les,

who lived on the nearest ranch. Dad was showing them the new mare. He wore dirty jeans and a faded shirt with the elbow worn through. If he didn't hurry, he wouldn't have time to clean up before Miss Miller came. As Molly watched, he lifted the horse's muzzle and opened her mouth so the Claypools could see her teeth.

You already showed them once, Dad. They know how old she is.

Molly lifted the dish towel and looked at the dough, divided into round floury balls for the rolls. They were rising nicely and as soon as Miss Miller came, she'd pop them into the oven. Everything was as ready as it could be, except for her father. She saw him and Mr. Claypool running their hands down the mare's forelegs. Les stood back a little, hands jammed in his pockets, broad shoulders hunched high.

They might fiddle around for another hour if she didn't do something. She sighed and went outside. Mr. Claypool grinned when he saw her coming. He hitched at his jeans, which hung precariously low on his bony hips while his stomach bulged out above. His pants always seemed about ready to slip off.

"You're looking mighty pretty today, young lady. Won't be long until all the boys are chasing after you. Right, Les?"

Les grunted and curled up his lip a little farther.

The left side of his mouth was always lifted just a little, and Molly thought he looked like a dog about to snarl. She'd never understood why the high-school girls and the young women thought he was so good-looking. He seemed sulky and stuck on himself to her.

Molly's father winked at her. She saw pride in his eyes and knew he thought she looked nice in the ruffled pink blouse she'd ordered from the Sears cata-log. The color went well with her brown eyes and hair, so dark that it was almost black. Molly stroked the horse's sleek neck and the mare turned to look at her in a friendly way.

"You're such a nice girl, Solita," she murmured.

"Solita. That's a pretty fancy name," said Mr. Claypool.

"She's a pretty fancy horse," Dad replied. "The fellow who named her said that Solita is Spanish for 'little sun.' "

Molly thought the name fit. The mare's coat was a bright golden sorrel, and she shone like burnished metal.

Dad went on. "She's half-thoroughbred. Look at those long legs."

"She may be a little fragile for this country, Jim."

"I don't think so. I've had her out a couple of times. I think she'll do."

/ 7 /

"It's getting late, Dad. Let me take Solita to the corral and that will save you a little time."

"I think Molly's hinting that I should hurry," he said. "She's invited Alison Edwards and their teacher for supper. She expects me to be presentable when they get here."

Mr. Claypool raised his eyebrows. "Ah, the lovely young Miss Miller. She's created quite a stir since she came last fall. Seems to me Les has noticed her, too."

Les grinned, his blue eyes gleaming. "She's hard to miss."

Molly didn't like it one bit that Les thought her teacher was pretty. At one time or another, he'd dated almost every young single woman who lived anywhere near. Miss Miller was too special for someone like him. Molly could hardly resist telling him so, but she knew it wouldn't be polite. She frowned and turned her head so that she wouldn't have to look at his self-satisfied face.

Dad patted her shoulder. "You go finish supper. I'll look after Solita and be right in."

He was soon showered and changed. He smelled of soap and was as lean and flat-bellied as a boy in his new jeans. His black hair was damp and feathery.

"You look nice," she told him as he raised the pot lid to smell the stew.

Molly's father put his hand over his heart and bowed in a courtly way. The radio was playing and a lively waltz filled the room. He lifted the hot pad out of Molly's hand and tossed it on the counter. He took her in his arms and they danced around the kitchen. He was light-footed and catlike even in his high-heeled cowboy boots. He whistled the tune along with the radio. Father and daughter dipped and turned together until the song was done. He bowed again. Molly curtsied. Then he handed the hot pad to her.

"Back to business," he said, smiling.

Miss Miller arrived a few minutes later. She'd picked up Alison, Molly's best friend, on the way. Suddenly Molly felt nervous. She flung open the front door.

"Hello, Miss Miller. Hello, Alison." Her voice sounded high-pitched and artificial. She cleared her throat as she ushered them into the living room.

Molly watched closely as Dad and her teacher shook hands a little stiffly. They'd met several times during the year: back-to-school night, the Christmas play, and other activities, but this was different. Miss Miller was all dressed up in a full skirt and very high heels that made her nearly as tall as Molly's father. Her curly light-brown hair looked as if she'd just washed it, and she kept smiling, showing a deep dimple in each cheek. Dad was using his company manners and now and then he glanced at Molly as if to ask if he were doing what she expected of him.

Molly bustled around bringing in iced tea. Then she sat on the edge of a chair with her feet crossed at the ankles. She held a cold glass, wrapped in a slippery paper napkin, in both hands. She and Alison listened as the adults made polite conversation about the weather, the school, and the road repairs that caused the thirty-mile trip to town to take even longer than usual.

Things got better after they went to the table. Miss Miller complained that Molly was ruining her diet, but she ate two rolls and took a second helping of stew just the same.

"Molly and Alison are my prize pupils, the best students in the sixth grade," she said. "And just look at the wonderful dinner that Molly cooked all by herself. Not many eleven-year-old girls could do as well. You must be very proud of her, Mr. Parker."

"I think she'll do. And call me Jim. Mr. Parker makes me feel older than I am."

"Oh, you're not old, Mr. Par . . . Jim." Miss Miller giggled and her cheeks turned pink.

"I'm thirty-eight," he said, looking downcast, but Molly could see that his eyes were smiling.

After everyone had finished the dessert, Molly

stood up. "Dad, why don't you take Miss Miller out so she can see Solita?"

Molly and Alison watched out the window as the two adults walked to the corral.

"Do you think they like each other?" Molly asked.

"I don't know. It's hard to tell with Miss Miller. She's always smiling and laughing. And I can't tell about your dad, either. He has such good manners. He'd be nice to anyone."

Molly scraped the plates and rinsed them. "I hope they like each other. Oh, I really hope they do."

"Don't hope too much," Alison said. "Last Saturday I saw Miss Miller having ice cream with Les Claypool."

Molly paused with a plate in her hand. Alison's eyes looked big and soft behind her glasses. Molly knew she'd hated to tell her friend that.

"Well, you know Les. He's always chasing women."

"Or they're chasing him."

"I just don't believe Miss Miller could like Les very much, especially now that she knows my dad a little better. Did you see the way she blushed when she called him Jim? Let's hurry and get the dishes done. We'll go up to my room so they can be alone down here. But first I'll light the fire. It's not too late in the spring for a fire in the evening, and I think a fireplace is romantic, don't you?"

Alison looked at her with a little smile. "You think of everything, don't you?"

Molly grinned back. "I try."

/ TWO /

"Do you like Miss Miller?"

Molly's father took another sip of breakfast coffee. "Yes, I think she's very nice."

"She's like that all the time. Always smiling and laughing even when there's nothing really funny. All the kids at school just love her."

"I'm not surprised to hear that she's popular."

"Since you like her so much and I know she liked you, too, let's invite her for next weekend. Maybe she could come after school on Friday and—"

"Wait a minute, Molly. Gayle is a likable young woman, but probably the most important word in that sentence is *young*. She's just out of college. This is her first teaching job. I doubt she's interested in seeing much of a man my age."

"I heard her tell you she didn't think you were

old. Besides, lots of men marry women much younger than—"

"*Marry!* Whoa-doggie! I've only met the woman two or three times at school before last night. Aren't you rushing things a little?"

Molly knew she'd made a mistake. "I didn't mean that you two should get married," she said quickly. "I just meant that people can really get along sometimes, even if they are different ages. Do you want some more hotcakes?"

Dad shook his head and looked at her thoughtfully. "I know this is a lonely life for you. Living this far out on a ranch is sometimes tough on a grown woman, and you're only a kid. You don't fuss or complain, so I'm likely to forget how much of the time you're alone."

"I love it here," she said truthfully. "It's just that now and then I think how nice it would be to have someone else here. Especially when you're out working around the ranch somewhere and the house is empty when I come home from school." She didn't want Dad to think that she was trying to make him feel sorry for her, so she added, "You'd have company, too. You're alone even more than I am."

The ranch house was more than a mile off the county road. Molly thought it would be company to see cars going by, even if they didn't stop. But the road was out of sight behind a curve of the hills and the only cars she saw were the few that came to their place. Sometimes she thought that if everyone else in the world disappeared, it would be days before she and Dad knew it, at least as far as sight was concerned.

The Claypools, their nearest neighbors, were over ten miles away by car, a little less than seven by horseback if a rider followed the cattle trail this side of the river. Mrs. Claypool came once a month to lend a hand with house cleaning. Molly looked forward to her arrival. She was a cheerful grandmotherly woman, good company as well as a big help.

Other ranches were even farther away. Alison lived more than halfway to town, at the end of a two-mile lane leading back off the county road. The long distances between the houses and the constant demands of ranch work meant that the families didn't visit one another very often. Because of this, it seemed like a special event when they did get together.

For the Parkers and others like them, the radio was the most important link to the rest of the world. It brought weather reports, local news, music, the sound of other voices into their homes. Their old television set got good reception on one channel, but the other signals were too weak and too far away to bring in programs that they could watch.

Molly went on with her thoughts. "Sometimes in the winter when the wind blows—there's something about the way the wind sounds at night."

"Yes, there is something about the wind. It can get to you. I've heard that a few of the early pioneer women actually went crazy, listening to the wind. They heard voices in it, or came to believe that the wind was some sort of living thing."

"Don't worry, Dad. I won't go crazy. I was born out here. I know it's only wind."

"And I was born here, too, so it should be in your blood. But still—no child should be alone as much as you've been."

He looked out the big window by the table, and Molly followed his gaze. There was a little knoll near the house. Molly's mother had loved trees, and at her request, Dad had planted three Lombardy poplars and a honey locust on the knoll. She'd scattered tulip and daffodil bulbs beneath the trees and planted them where they fell. Most of the daffodils were through blooming, but the tulips still showed brave and bright—red, white, and yellow against the grass.

Her father's greenish eyes grew distant and looked at something, or someone, far beyond the tulips and the little grove. Molly's thoughts followed him back in time to the woman who had planted the flowers.

Molly had been five years old when her mother died. A drunk driver had smashed head-on into the car carrying Mrs. Claypool, Molly's mother, and the child who would have been Molly's little sister if she'd lived long enough to be born. Mrs. Claypool was the only survivor.

Sometimes it was difficult for Molly to tell what she really remembered and what she only imagined about her mother. Photographs showed a young woman with a serious mouth and dark eyes, like Molly's, looking directly into the camera. When Molly remembered her mother, it was always in a sort of dreamy ochre light as if in a photograph taken long ago and left in a trunk for years.

Molly's most often recalled memory—one she knew had really happened, was of a hot day during the last summer her mother had lived. She held Molly on the saddle in front of her, and they rode to the river not far from the Palisades. These were cliffs that rose up above the water for nearly one hundred feet, as straight as if they had been sheared off by a gigantic knife. The water was deep and swift at the base of the cliffs just before it plunged in white foam through the rapids beyond. But a short way upriver, where Molly and her mother went, the river was shallow and the current gentle.

They left the horse on the bank, took off their

shoes and slowly waded into the water. The river bottom had been gritty and sharp with gravel under Molly's bare feet, but the water felt cool after the hot sun. They'd laughed and splashed each other. Finally Mother plunged full-length into the shallow water, clothes and all. Molly followed and they rolled over, laughing.

Molly remembered when her mother sat up, brushing her long, wet hair out of her eyes. All laughter left her face, to be replaced by a look of wonder.

"Look, Molly," she said softly.

A white horse stood on the opposite bank, glossy in the afternoon sun. Maybe it was the way the light shone on him, but for a moment he looked like a statue, larger than life, all of his powerful muscles deeply defined as if he were carved out of marble. He watched the two people, his eyes intent, his ears thrust sharply forward, as if curious about what they were doing.

"Just look at him. It's the Ghost."

The stallion tossed his head so that his long mane rippled like water. He pivoted on his hind feet and moved along the edge of the river, hoofs lifting in a springy trot. But he was still curious and paused to look at them again with large dark eyes.

"Remember this moment, Molly. You may never

see him again, but remember that once you saw the Ghost."

The wild horse turned and trotted away into one of the canyons. In a few moments, he had disappeared from sight.

Her mother's eyes shone with delight. "Wasn't he wonderful? I know you've heard the stories about him. There was a ghost when I was your age, a big beautiful white stallion that lived out in the badlands. Old ranchers used to tell me that even he wasn't the first, that there's always been a ghost horse across the river.

"Common sense tells me that it can't possibly be the same horse. But yet no ordinary stallion could pass on his looks to his colt so completely that each offspring—if that's what they are—seems to look just like his father. There's something very unusual, very strange about that horse. But whatever he is, I love to think that he still lives out there somewhere. And I hope he always does."

The cat, Velvet, put her paws on Molly's leg and the touch returned the girl to the present. Velvet gazed up with eyes as green as grapes. Molly stroked her glossy black head and gave her a bite of pancake. Dad shifted in his chair and looked at his daughter, coming back from wherever he had been.

"I'm going to take a ride as soon as I do the

dishes," Molly said briskly. "Cappy hasn't been out all week and he needs some exercise."

"Okay. You wash. I'll dry." For a moment, it seemed as if he might say more, but instead he began to clear the table.

Cappy was glad to be out and moving. He trotted briskly along, playing with the bit in his mouth. He rolled his eyes at every movement, hoping for an excuse to shy. They went to the river, about three quarters of a mile from the house. Some of her father's cattle were drinking at the ford. They raised their heads, muzzles dripping, and watched as Cappy splashed through the water. Molly turned the horse upstream.

Dad had said that Miss Miller was too young for him, but he'd called her Gayle this morning. Molly realized that she would have to be careful not to rush them too much, but maybe, by next winter, they'd be married. Miss Miller—only by then Molly, too, would call her Gayle—would drive her home after they both finished school. They'd cook supper together, and she'd show Gayle how to make Dad's favorite pecan cookies. Miss Miller—it was still too hard to say Gayle—would laugh and tease and even an ordinary thing like making cookies would be so much fun.

After Dad came in, they'd build a fire in the fireplace and all sit there together. Her father would play his harmonica—the sad slow cowboy laments, the happy she'll-be-comin'-round-the-mountain tunes, and the freight train song where he made the harmonica wail *waaa-waaah,* just like the distant sound of a train passing in the night. Molly and Miss Miller would sing, and none of them would even notice the melancholy wind as it cried around the house.

A faint game trail led off to the right, going into one of the dry gulches that wound into the rough country south of the river. Molly turned Cappy in that direction. After awhile, the trail angled up out of the gulch and disappeared in rocks and sand on a flat-topped ridge. Her horse moved along briskly as if he knew where he was going, and Molly let him have his head.

Soon she saw the bones of a cow, picked clean by coyotes and carrion-eating birds. Molly guessed it was winter-kill and had died during the heavy blizzard they'd had a year ago in March. A patch of buttercups bloomed among the remains, their shiny yellow heads seeming to festoon the white bones like decorations.

She got off Cappy, dropped the reins to ground tie him, and stepped a little closer. The skull was tipped upside down, probably left that way by an animal. Molly turned it back over with her foot. She walked twice around the skeleton, intrigued by the way one kind of life had sprung up in the place of another's dying.

The girl stepped backward to take another look and there, no more than two feet from her, was a rattlesnake. It lay flat, its body slightly curved, its triangular head barely lifted off the ground. She must have nearly stepped on it several times as she walked around the skeleton. The snake watched her and, as if knowing it had been discovered, flickered its tongue in and out of its mouth.

Swiftly, Molly picked up a big rock and prepared to smash it down on the snake, to crush its ugly head. The rattler watched without moving. Molly stood with her hands upraised, clutching the rock. The snake hadn't hurt her. It had lain right there and let her practically step on it. It could easily have bitten her. Wouldn't it be cruel and ungrateful to kill the reptile when it had left her alone? Molly dropped the rock and moved slowly away. The snake followed her with its head as she mounted Cappy. By the time her horse had gone a few paces, the rattler blended into the ground, and she couldn't see it any more.

The ridge soon ended, dropping steeply into another gulch. This would be a rough descent and

Molly paused on the brink to consider if she wanted to go on. Ahead of her, craggy rocks stood out like castle turrets on the ridges. Deep twisting canyons wound in endless mazes in between. Dad didn't like her to ride in that country which stretched away, wild and treacherous, without a ranch or a road for a hundred miles.

Suddenly Cappy pricked his ears and swung his head to the right. He snorted nervously. Molly followed his gaze and saw a tall white horse on the next ridge. He appeared like a figure in a fairy tale, outlined against the castlelike crags behind him. It was the Ghost, she knew at once, the same horse that she and her mother had seen by the river. Once again, Molly and the Ghost regarded one another. He was as beautiful as she remembered.

All too soon, he moved away and vanished out of sight below the top of the ridge.

Elation surged through the girl and she laughed out loud. *He was still there.* Oh, she was glad to know that he still ran free beyond the ropes and the corrals. *Mother, do you know he's still out there?*

She knew this sighting had been given to her as a gift, an exchange because she had let the rattlesnake live. If a butterfly had lit on the ground at her feet, it would have been easy to let the delicate creature go. It's easy to spare the beautiful things, easy to kill the

ugly ones like snakes. But she and the rattlesnake had met and gone their separate ways in peace. The tenuous thread that connects all living things to one another had been unbroken. Each had given a gift to the other; now hers had been doubled when the Ghost stood on the hill.

/ THREE /

Molly was an October child, born in that month of falling leaves and blowing winds. Sometimes it seemed the bitter October wind haunted her all the rest of the year. In spite of what she'd told her father, she did sometimes feel that the wind had a life and a will of its own and that it wasn't always friendly.

Her mother had died on a windy November night only a little more than a month after her fifth birthday. Molly remembered sitting at the small kitchen table. She ate toast and drank hot chocolate that her father had made for her. It was already dark, much later than it should have been, and Mother was not yet home from her trip to town to see the doctor. Dad didn't sit down; he kept pacing to the window to look down the lane and then back to look at the clock. The dry wind moaned around the house as it rushed by on its long journey from no place to no-where.

"Here she comes. Thank God," Dad said, his voice light with relief.

Molly went to the window and looked at the car lights coming slowly toward the house. She still felt leaden with fear and her mouth hurt where she'd burned it on the hot chocolate. Her father flung open the door and his shadow fell out into the yard, black in a golden rectangle. When the car's door opened and its interior lights went on, both of them saw, not Molly's mother, but two state patrolmen getting out of a police car.

Now, six years later, Molly lay in her upstairs bed-room and listened to the wind. It was a warm, bois-terous wind of early June, not the bleak wind of autumn; but still there was something foreboding in its sound. It had blown almost constantly during the three days school had been out for the summer.

Molly had managed to get Miss Miller out to the ranch one more time. They'd gone horseback riding, but it hadn't been a success. Miss Miller was afraid of horses. Dad had been patient as she giggled and bounced awkwardly in the saddle, clutching the horn and hauling on her horse's tender mouth.

"I'll learn to ride," she'd said. "I really want to learn."

But now that school was out and they didn't see

each other every day, it wouldn't be easy for Molly to keep inviting Miss Miller out. She wanted to suggest to her father that he ask her to the Saturday night dance at the Grange Hall, but was afraid that he would refuse.

The wind gusted so loudly that it seemed as if the roof would be pulled off. Through the open bedroom window, Molly could hear the horses whinnying out in the corral. The wind blew against the opposite side of the house, so her window was sheltered and didn't have to be closed during the warm night. The wind, or something, made the horses nervous because she had heard them several times before.

Her father's room was downstairs and on the other side of the house. He might not be able to hear the horses. Molly stumbled from the bed and looked out. There was enough moonlight so that she could see the shapes of the animals in the corral. All at once, as if turned off by a switch, the wind dropped to a breeze. The sudden change seemed almost unnatural. Molly listened but couldn't hear anything except the faint rustle of trees and bushes near the house. The horses were quiet now that the fierce gusts had slackened.

She got back into bed and felt around the foot until she found the cat. Velvet's body seemed as limp and boneless as a stuffed toy as the girl pulled her across the blanket. She snuggled the cat against her and Velvet purred sleepily under her chin. Molly fell asleep and dreamed.

In her dream, she rode horseback with Dad and Miss Miller. It was a beautiful summer day. All the colors seemed unusually bright, as if they were in a technicolor movie. The grass was long and green; the trail beneath their feet was white and free of dust. Both sides of the path were lined with trees whose thick dark leaves turned and trembled in the breeze.

After awhile they came to a stream and paused to let the horses drink. Another horse whinnied off in the distance. Cappy flung up his head, water dripping from his mouth, and answered. A wonderful white stallion came out of the trees. It was the Ghost, and Molly knew that he'd come to visit her. She took an apple from her jacket pocket and slipped down from Cappy. She waded across the stream and the Ghost whickered at her, tossing his head eagerly up and down. She held out the apple and he lowered his head to take it from her hand.

Suddenly the dream seemed to change, and now Molly was lying in bed. It was almost morning. She could tell by the dim gray light coming from outside.

I wonder if the Ghost is still here, she thought.

She slipped out of bed and went to the window. It was quiet outside, everything motionless and hushed as the first thin split of yellowish light began to separate night from day. Only Solita circled restlessly around and around in the corral. Cappy and Ranger, the other gelding, crowded together in the center. Solita stopped and stared off to the south, toward the low-rising hills still invisible in the darkness. The two geldings followed her gaze, working their ears nervously back and forth.

Molly heard Solita snort softly. The mare danced a few steps and then turned to face southward again. A shadow moved among other shadows outside the corral. A loose rock clicked gently against another, the sound drifting faintly through the open window.

The Ghost emerged from the dawn, tall and pale as the vanished moon. He floated around the outside of the corral, sometimes almost brushing against the poles. He pranced like a show horse, lifting his feet high, neck arched, mane and tail pluming out like smoke. Solita swiveled to face him.

Molly's mind was foggy. Her thoughts moved with leaden slowness. She wondered if she could find another apple for the Ghost. Her hands fumbled for the pockets in her jacket, but the pockets weren't where they belonged.

She heard the Ghost seeming to speak to Solita in

urgent snorts and deep rumbling whinnies. He pressed against the fence, reaching toward the mare. He kept leaning, pushing harder and harder, until the poles groaned in protest. He pawed with his front hoofs, tearing up chunks of earth. He half-reared and smashed his massive chest against the bars. One of them cracked. The three horses inside galloped around in a frenzy of excitement and fear.

The fabric beneath Molly's hands felt soft, unlike the stiff denim of her jacket. She looked down at her front. She wore her white pajamas with little blue flower sprigs on them.

I'm not dreaming. This is really happening.

She looked up as the Ghost lunged against the weakened pole, battering it with tremendous force. Molly rushed to the top of the stairs.

"Dad! Dad!" she screamed. "Wake up! The Ghost is after Solita."

She ran back to the window in time to see the broken pole topple to the ground. The stallion leaped into the corral and rushed at the other horses. His long neck stretched out, weaving in a serpentlike movement, as the tame horses retreated.

Molly grabbed her jeans off a chair and jammed one leg into them. She hopped across the floor to the bedroom door.

"Dad, did you hear me?"

Her father yelled something from downstairs. Molly pulled on the other pant leg, stuffing her pajamas inside. She dashed back to the window for another quick look and saw the Ghost nip and shove until he had separated Solita from the geldings. He crowded her toward the broken fence. The mare plunged over the top and raced toward the ranch house. The stallion forged ahead and jostled against her, turning her toward the southern hills.

Molly ran downstairs, still in her pajama top. When she reached the porch, her father was nearly at the corral, pulling at his pants with one hand and clutching his rifle with the other. Molly followed him as fast as she could, but she hadn't put on any shoes. Sharp stones and other hard things jabbed into her winter-tender feet, slowing her down.

Dad caught Ranger and threw his saddle onto the horse's back. He didn't bother to open the gate, but urged the horse to leap over the broken pole. They galloped off full speed through the first dawn light. Off in the distance, Molly glimpsed an ash-white horse and Solita running side by side as they streaked away toward the river and the badlands beyond.

There was no time for a saddle and bridle. Molly grabbed a short rope, slipped a loop over Cappy's neck and then twisted another loop around his muzzle to form a makeshift halter. She swung up on him bareback and set off after her father.

As Molly neared the river, the ridges on the other side emerged like darker shadows through the gray of morning. Even though it was not full daylight, the rolling open countryside made it easy for her to see a long way in all directions. Ahead of her father, Solita and the Ghost neared the crest of a rise. Solita ran hard with the white stallion right on her heels. She slowed down and the Ghost nipped her on the haunch. She flicked her tail and surged ahead. The mare topped the ridge and dropped out of sight on the other side.

The Ghost whirled on the crest and looked back the way he had come. Molly's father raised his rifle and sighted along the barrel. Shock struck her with the force of a lightning bolt. Was he going to shoot the Ghost?

As she watched, too surprised and dismayed even to call out, he lowered the rifle and reined to a halt. He lifted the rifle again and aimed carefully.

"Dad!" Molly cried.

Even as she spoke, she saw the Ghost toss his head so that his long silvery mane shimmered. Then he spun around and seemed to vanish as if a wind had picked him up and whisked him away. There hadn't even been time for her father to pull the trigger. He glanced over his shoulder at Molly, then kicked

Ranger in the ribs and dashed on in pursuit. When Dad reached the ridge top where the Ghost had paused, he pulled up once more and Molly finally caught up with him.

There were no horses to be seen. Below them, the river looked gray and flat in the early morning light. The water didn't appear to move. Neither did anything else, except a silent-winged owl heading home to its cranny in the rocks. Molly could see the shadowy openings of half a dozen little canyons twisting away into the badlands. She knew that Solita and the stallion had disappeared into one of them.

"Ghost, you old devil!" The words exploded out of her father. Ranger flinched and jumped ahead at the angry sound. Dad checked him, patted his neck and tried to soothe the gelding as he wheeled and danced restlessly.

"Are we going on?" Molly asked. She felt jumpy and excited like Ranger. Part of her didn't want the chase to end so soon. That part wanted to go thundering down the slope and gallop into one of the canyons, to follow the Ghost as far as they could go. But another part of her was afraid of what might happen if they again came in sight of the stallion. The rifle was back in her father's scabbard, but it might not stay there.

Dad answered her question. "It's no use chasing

the horses anymore this morning. That's hostile country out there, and the Ghost knows it better than we do. It's his home—his and the rattlesnakes and the coyotes."

Molly knew what it was like across the river. Tracks would be difficult to find in the hard-rock canyons. Even if they did find a trail that they could follow for awhile, by afternoon the wind was sure to blow, and drifting sand and grit would soon scour out any faint tracks which might otherwise be found.

"Dad, were you really going to shoot the Ghost?"

"I suppose I would have, but I couldn't get a bead on him with Ranger running over such rough ground. And after I stopped, the Ghost disappeared too quick."

"Mother wouldn't have wanted you to kill him," Molly said in a small voice.

"I know. Your mother always did like fairy tales and happy endings. Let's go home, kid."

They rode in silence. Molly felt her father looking at her. "I really didn't want to shoot him," he said, sounding apologetic. "But I was madder than a wet hornet."

"I know that you hate to lose Solita, but isn't there a way you can get her back without shooting the Ghost?"

"Maybe."

They jogged along for awhile. Molly felt her system slowing down, the tension and excitement seeping out of her. She yawned.

Dad spoke again. "When you told me that you'd seen the Ghost a few days ago, I thought it was some other horse, some stray the same color. It's been a couple of years since he's come across the river, and I thought maybe the old son of a gun was dead by now. Lord knows he should be, but then he's never done things the way most animals do, even die. He's some kind of horse."

Her father's voice was half-admiring, and Molly was glad that he, too, recognized that the Ghost was a special creature.

He went on. "I think there might be another way to go after him, a better way."

"How's that?"

"As soon as we get home, I'm going to call Chick Bartlett and ask him to fly out and look for the horses in his little Piper Cub. When he locates the herd, we'll get the Claypools and Roy Edwards and some of the others. Then we'll have us a wild horse chase with the odds on our side."

"It doesn't seem fair to chase the Ghost with an airplane," Molly said.

"It isn't fair of him to steal people's mares, either.

He's got away with a lot over the years, but he's not getting away with Solita. She's valuable and a good horse. I like her, and I'm going to get her back."

Ghost, why did you do this to us? Molly wondered. *Why didn't you just stay out there where you belong?*

/ FOUR /

It was only a few days until Chick Bartlett reported that he'd located the herd. Jim Parker, the Claypools, Alison's father, and several other men rode out to a valley at the edge of the rough country where the Ghost ranged. Molly and Alison went along.

After camp was set up, the men began to build the corral. They'd selected a spot with scatterings of juniper and pinon trees. Some of the trees were dead. With ropes fastened from the trunks to their saddle horns, it was easy for the men to uproot the trees from the loose, shallow soil. The dead trees were dragged to the spot chosen for the corral and used to fill in open spaces between the living trees and brush. The stiff, twisted branches and trunks locked easily together. Dead logs and sometimes cut green branches were woven in. The corral sides were reinforced with rope in places.

Several jays hovered close by. They perched on the branches of trees or hopped around on the ground, seeming to take an interest in the construction. At mealtime, they darted in to pick up crumbs and scraps that the people dropped.

"We're not trying very hard to hide this trap," Jim Parker explained to Molly and Alison. "In the old days, when wild horses were chased only by men on horseback, sometimes they'd build wings—barriers—as long as a quarter of a mile, extending way out on both sides and gradually funneling down to the corral. The wings were carefully camouflaged. All tracks and signs of man were erased so that the wild horses wouldn't get suspicious and bolt off. It'll be a lot easier today with the airplane. We don't have to run our own horses into the ground rounding up the wild ones. Chick will do that for us, and our horses will be fresh when the wild ones are all tired out."

It's not fair, Molly thought again, but she kept it to herself this time. She didn't want the men to think her foolish and sentimental, like a city girl who thought that all wild horses were magnificent creatures that should never be touched. Molly knew that many of them were scrubby, stunted, and undernourished.

Once on a trip to Denver, Molly had looked into an alley and seen a family of stray cats, a mother and three half-grown kittens. They were sunning themselves on a pile of boxes. The cats were thin with dull, patchy fur and too-large eyes. They were half the size of plump, sleek Velvet back home. The cats stared tensely at Molly when she paused, ready to run and hide if she took a step into the alley.

Many wild horses were no more attractive and no better fed than the stray cats. Thinning the herds would benefit the horses who stayed on the range. The country where they lived was so poor that it could support only a limited number of wild horses.

But the Ghost was different. He was a majestic creature and everyone knew it. It was clear from the way people talked about him. And soon he would be herded by a noisy machine into a corral, the first time in his life that he'd ever been confined.

Molly's feelings were all mixed up. She wanted her father to get Solita back, and it was exciting to think about seeing the Ghost again. Yet she didn't want him caught and tamed like any other horse, all his beauty and mystery turned ordinary. Dad had avoided answering when she'd asked him what he planned to do with the stallion if they caught him. She had the feeling that he didn't really know, that he was intent on recovering Solita and hadn't thought much beyond that. But maybe they wouldn't catch the Ghost after all. If any horse could get away from an airplane, he could.

Her thoughts went around and around like a coyote she'd seen once, kept in a little cage at a gas station out in the desert. Then she'd thought that the coyote was probably crazy, and now she was beginning to feel that way herself. Molly sighed and took her tin plate to the creek where she scoured it with sand and rinsed it in the running water.

The corral was nearly finished just after noon on the second day. Chick Bartlett flew overhead in his red and white Piper Cub. He would use his airplane to herd the horses to the valley. He circled twice around the camp, high enough so that he wouldn't frighten the cow ponies. Dad waved his hat and pointed west in the direction the pilot had seen the wild horses.

"Go get 'em," he yelled, just as though the man in the airplane could hear him. Bartlett waggled his wings and flew off over the hills.

The men had built the temporary corral just before the place where the valley funneled down to a narrow canyon. Mr. Claypool lay on the ground, taking a break from cutting and piling the last of the brush. He puffed on his pipe, one eye closed against the smoke. His stomach mounded up like a bag of grain. Les sat nearby with his back against a tree.

"Don't get your hopes up too high, Jim," the

older Claypool warned. "Lots of men have chased the Ghost and none of them have ever caught him. Using an airplane is a pretty smart idea, but that old horse has been around a long time, and he's pretty smart, too."

"I've heard about him all my life," Les said. "As old as he must be by now, it's a wonder he can even run anymore."

"Seems that way, don't it?" his father agreed. "Why, even when I was a boy, fifty years ago, there was stories about the Ghost. He stole mares from my daddy. My daddy chased him and I've chased him before, like half the cowboys around here. But nobody ever caught him, never even got a rope on him. He's called the Ghost for more than one reason."

A shiver ran through Molly, that feeling of prickly apprehension that comes in the middle of a dark night. She looked at Alison and saw her friend looking back, chewing on her long brown hair the way she did when she was nervous.

"Do you mean he's a real *ghost?*" Alison asked. "Not a regular horse?"

Mr. Claypool puffed away without answering and Molly turned to her father. He grinned a little. "Color can be passed down. It seems likely that this Ghost had a grandpappy, the same as we did, and he could very well have been white, too."

Molly didn't know if she were disappointed or not. Ever since her mother had first told her about the Ghost, it gave her a cold chill to think of a phantom horse living out on the edge of the beyond, now and then drifting in close to the ranches. The three times she'd seen the stallion she knew that he was real, but sometimes when she thought about him she wasn't so sure.

"Well, we'll see how it goes," Mr. Claypool said, shifting his stomach to a more comfortable position. "Maybe he's not a spooky-type ghost, but he sure ain't any regular horse, either."

Toward the middle of the afternoon, they heard the airplane coming back. Once again, it circled the camp and then flew back the way it had come.

"They're coming. Get ready," Dad said.

They all mounted their horses and took their positions along both sides of the valley. Molly and Alison hurried to the hill at the upper end where they would have a good view of everything. Soon the airplane came buzzing back. It flew so low that it looked as though a tall man could almost reach up and touch it from the ridge tops. It didn't fly in a straight line but looped and circled, climbed and dove, darting this way and that like a red and white dragonfly.

"He's herding the horses," Molly said.

"It's sure a lot easier than doing it on horseback," Alison murmured.

"It doesn't seem right to me. The Ghost could outrun another horse, but no animal can get away from an airplane."

"Do you want him to get away? Don't you want to catch him?"

Molly didn't answer.

In a few minutes, a faint cloud of dust rose behind one of the near ridges. Then the horses topped the crest and poured like an avalanche down the slope. The lead mare was nearly as black and shiny as Molly's cat. Following the mare was a surging mass of color—bay, sorrel, pinto, gray, and buckskin. There were more than a dozen horses in all as well as several colts.

"There he is. There's the Ghost," Alison cried as the last horse, a white one, came over the hill.

"Look, there's Solita." Molly pointed. Excitement rose in her as the horses spilled out into the valley. It was impossible not to get caught up in the action. The lead mare spotted one of the riders waiting in the valley and swerved back toward the hills. The airplane darted after her, diving close over her head, and sent her plunging down into the center of the valley.

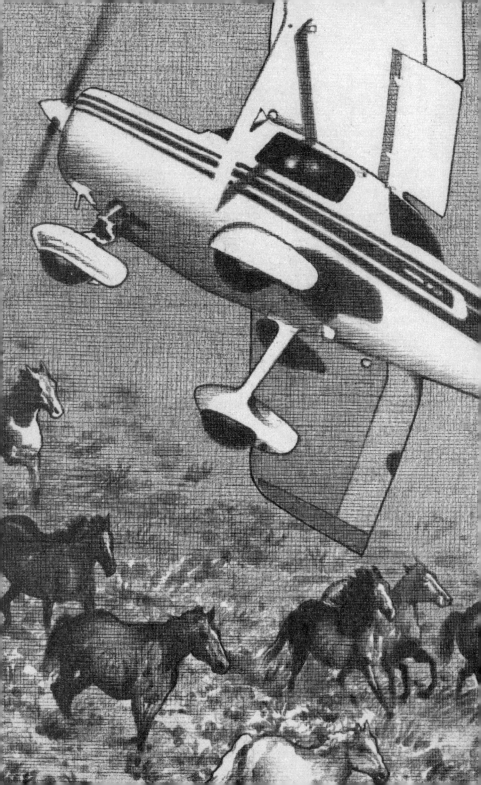

Even at this distance Molly could see that the horses' coats were dark with sweat. The Ghost kept close behind them, bringing up the rear to protect them if he could. The herd raced full tilt down the valley, while the mounted men sat on both sides, watching.

/ FIVE /

As the horses neared the far end of the valley where the corral had been built, the airplane rose and swept ahead. It circled and roared down at the animals, forcing them to double back the way they had come. Bartlett was tiring them out so they'd be easier to hold in the makeshift corral. The horses galloped back toward Molly and Alison. Their gait was labored, slower than it had been. As they came closer, the girls could see the lead mare's eyes, wild and white-ringed with fear.

Once again, the Piper Cub roared out in front. Molly saw the pilot through the window as he banked almost directly in front of the girls. Cappy flinched and whirled away. Molly got him turned around in time to see the pilot swoop down at the other horses. The mares scattered in different directions. The Ghost increased his stride, trying to round them up, to get them back under his control. The airplane, droning over his head, confused and frightened him.

Two of the mares bolted away from the herd. The pilot let them go. A waiting rider roped one of the horses. The other one, a brown and white pinto, put on a burst of speed and streaked away in another direction. A man on a big roan horse went tearing in pursuit. The pinto plunged down a creek bank, splashed through the shallow water, and lunged up the opposite bank with the rider following behind.

"Look at that crazy Les," Alison said. "He rides like a wild man."

They tore through the willow brush, leaped a fallen log, and scrambled across a rocky slope—wild horse and wild rider hot on her heels. Loose rocks went clattering downward as they flashed out of sight around the curve of the hill.

"He'll kill himself one of these days," Alison muttered.

Molly and Alison turned their attention back to the valley. By now several horses had slowed, stumbling with exhaustion. The waiting men roped them. Two members of the herd had to be ranch raised because they stopped and stood quietly the instant they felt the ropes on their necks. Molly watched as her father sent his horse galloping across the valley. He threw a loop over Solita's head. She halted, head down, obviously tired. He got off his mount and went over to stroke her neck and run his hands over her legs to make sure she was all right. The wild horses were terrified, confused and worn out with running. One by one, they were forced into the corral.

Finally, only the Ghost was still outside. He charged back and forth in front of the opening, first in one direction and then the other. The riders whooped, waving ropes and hats. The airplane howled overhead, scaring the cow ponies nearly as much as the wild ones.

Molly's stomach kept doing flip-flops. Her eyes felt dry and strained.

The Ghost will do something now, she thought. *Something surprising and wonderful. He won't let himself get caught.*

As if hearing her thoughts, the Ghost wheeled and thundered straight at the riders. They closed ranks. One of the men pulled a pistol and emptied it into the air. A rifle shot sounded somewhere in the distance. The Piper Cub came swooping down. The Ghost whirled again and galloped through the entrance to the corral. The men cheered.

"They got him." Molly's voice sounded flat. That

was exactly the way she felt inside, dull and flat with disbelief.

Alison stood up in her stirrups and looked around. "Did you hear that other shot? It sounded like a rifle."

"Yeah, I heard it. One of the men got excited, I suppose."

"I think it came from somewhere else, but I couldn't tell where."

"What does it matter? They got the Ghost."

"You're right. Let's go down and see him."

"You go ahead. I'll be down in a minute," Molly said.

"What's the matter with you?"

"Nothing's the matter. I just want to watch from up here a little longer."

"You can see better down there." Alison waited a moment, but when Molly didn't respond, she turned her horse and trotted away.

Chick Bartlett made a final circle with the airplane and then headed toward home. Several riders waved at him as he flew off. The men below closed the opening to the makeshift corral by pulling tarps strung on ropes across it. The horses could have forced their way out if they had tried, but a wild horse didn't know that and wouldn't try to push its way through what appeared to be a solid wall. The mares milled around the corral for a few minutes and then halted, too tired to move anymore. Molly could see the white shape that was the Ghost as he still circled restlessly around and around.

She didn't know how much time passed while she sat there, unwilling to go down and see the Ghost in captivity. She saw Alison and her father talking together, then both of them turned and Alison pointed at her. She felt a moment's anxiety, afraid that Dad would ride up to see why she wasn't celebrating with the rest. But he seemed to be busy, so maybe she would be left alone.

After awhile she glimpsed movement across the creek about a quarter of a mile away. A strange figure came lurching through the sagebrush. It appeared to be two-legged and had a great hump on its back. It moved slowly, unevenly. Half a dozen range cattle followed a little way behind. Molly stood up in her stirrups to get a better look.

The figure moved a few more steps and stopped. The hump on its back shifted and then she realized that it was a saddle, carried over a man's shoulder.

"Uh-oh," she said aloud. She touched Cappy with her heels and hurried in that direction. When she got closer, she recognized Les Claypool, limping steadily along. He paused and looked up when he heard her coming. The cattle stopped and looked at her, too, then went back to staring, goggle-eyed, at Les. His face was covered with sweat and he looked pasty gray beneath his tan.

"What happened?" she asked.

"Poor old Rusty put his foot in a hole and we took a bad spill, tail over teakettle. He broke his leg. I heard it snap, it was so loud. I had to shoot him. Poor old Rusty."

"Oh, I'm sorry. He was such a good horse."

"Yeah, I'll sure miss him." He lowered the saddle carefully to the ground, wincing as he did so. "Look at those dumb animals." He pointed at the cattle. "They been following me for at least a mile, eyes about ready to fall out of their heads. Range critters never see anybody except on horseback. They think I'm a whole new kind of animal."

Molly slipped to the ground. "Get on Cappy. I'll hand your saddle up to you."

Les took hold of her saddle horn and started to pull himself up. He made a sound—*"ugh!"*—as if someone had put a foot in his stomach. His lips turned white and he sagged against the side of the horse. Molly quickly put her arms around him, afraid he was going to collapse. He was so big that she probably couldn't hold him up, but she'd try.

"Darn it all, Molly. I can't do it." His voice sounded shaky.

/ 53 /

"Where do you hurt?"

"My left side and leg. I probably busted a couple of ribs. Don't know what I did to my leg."

"You wait here, and I'll go get help. Do you want to sit down?"

"I dunno. If I do, I may never get up again."

Just the same, he eased himself to the ground. Molly helped him as much as she could, then swung up on Cappy. The cattle were edging closer, eyes still fixed on Les. She didn't think they'd hurt him, but they might make him nervous, afraid he'd get stepped on. She rushed at them, yelling, and they bolted away. She chased them for a minute or two. It would take them awhile to get up courage enough to come back, even if their curiosity remained. By then she'd have returned with help.

She patted her horse's neck. "Come on, Cappy. Let's see how fast you can get to camp without putting your foot in a hole, too."

/ SIX /

It took only a few minutes for Molly to gallop down the valley and tell everyone what had happened. Vernon Claypool, Alison and her father, and Molly's father followed her back to where she'd left Les. The others stayed to watch the horses. The girls stood to one side as they examined the injured man.

Mr. Claypool took his pocket knife and slit the leg of Les's jeans from the hem to above his knee.

"It's starting to swell just above the boot. Looks like you busted it, boy."

"I'm not surprised to hear it. It's starting to hurt some."

"We don't have anything for pain except some aspirin. It won't help a whole lot, but you may as well take it," Jim Parker said. He dug around in his saddlebag and handed a small bottle and a canteen of water to Les.

"Maybe I better slit your boot, too," Les's father said. "It won't be too good if the leg starts swelling down inside."

Roy Edwards rode down to the trees and bushes that grew along the creek. He returned with two straight sticks about as thick as Molly's wrist.

"We'll use these for splints," he said. "Anybody want to volunteer a couple pieces of their rope to tie them on?"

"No need to cut a good rope," Jim Parker said. "We can use belts." He slipped his wide leather belt out of the loops.

Vernon Claypool did the same. "Mine will go around two or three times, at least. And you two girls stop your gigglin'. A big belly is the sign of a well-fed, contented man."

Les lay impassively as the men worked on him. Now and then he closed his eyes for a moment, but he didn't make a sound.

"I'll go back to the creek and cut some poles. We can make a travois," Roy Edwards said.

Les opened his eyes. "No travois!" Carefully he raised up on one elbow. "I'll ride a horse."

His father shook his head. "Not a good idea. You'll be a lot more comfortable layin' down."

"No travois," Les insisted. "You're not dragging me behind you like I was some elk you shot on a hunting trip. That jostling over rocks and bumps would kill me sure. You get me on a horse, and I'll ride it."

"Boy, you always was stubborn."

"I got it from my old man."

"You do look a little pale around the gills, Les," Jim Parker said. "Maybe you should listen to your dad."

"All this arguing is aggravating the pain. If I can't ride a horse home, you just plant me here."

"Oh, let him have his way." Mr. Claypool gave in. "If he can't ride old Sugarfoot, there ain't much hope for him, anyway. The horse is gentle enough so he can get on him from the right side and not have to step on his bad leg."

He led over his big bay gelding with the one white foot. The men helped Les get upright and into the saddle. He kept his right foot in the stirrup and let the other one hang stiffly in the splint.

"Vernon, you take my horse," Jim Parker said. "I'll ride with Molly."

Molly took her foot out of the left stirrup. Dad stepped into it and swung up behind her. Roy Edwards picked up Les's saddle. They made their way slowly down to the camp.

Finally Les was settled as comfortably as possible, lying on a blanket in the shade of a tree with his head on his saddle. It was nearly five o'clock in the evening, and would soon be too dark to travel. There wasn't anything for Molly to do and it seemed that she could no longer avoid looking at the Ghost. She walked slowly toward the enclosure.

The stallion stood quietly, but his head was up and eyes and ears alert. He watched her approach Close up, he was not white but a pale dappled gray.

"Ghost, do you remember me?"

He only glared at her.

Molly spoke softly. "I'm sorry they caught you, but you should never have taken Solita."

She thought of her mother and was glad that she wasn't here to see this stallion in a corral like any other horse. And yet he wasn't like the others. He was taller and heavier than the rest of his herd. Powerful muscles rippled under his shiny skin whenever he moved. When people approached the corral, he didn't retreat. He stood his ground, his eyes fierce and wary in a finely shaped head.

Molly's father came up beside her. "Look at those eyes. Sorta makes you glad there's a barrier between us, doesn't it?"

Molly nodded.

"We're going to leave at daybreak tomorrow morning, so we can get Les to the doctor as soon as possible. Right now we have to get a little control over the Ghost."

Alison's father approached, carrying his rope

coiled in his hand. "Let's get to it, Jim. You kids stay back out of the way."

The men all mounted and approached the corral. The wild mares and colts churned around in the middle while the Ghost stood still, watching.

"Jim, you get the first throw," Mr. Claypool said. "It was you that organized the chase."

Molly's father shook out a loop. He gave it a couple of turns and then sailed the rope gently over the Ghost's head. For an instant, the horse didn't move. His eyes stayed fixed on the man at the other end of the rope. Vernon Claypool, on the opposite side of the corral, was ready to make his toss. But before he could, the Ghost exploded into action with the suddenness of dynamite going off. His ears snapped back flat to his head. His mouth opened, baring big, dangerous-looking teeth. Soundless except for the drumming of his hoofs, he lunged straight at Jim Parker. His gelding, Ranger, trained to keep the rope taut, danced backwards.

"Watch him! He's gonna bust out!" somebody yelled.

Roy Edwards and two other men drove their horses toward the makeshift fence just as the Ghost hit it. Poles snapped and brush crackled as he tried to climb over. The men used their hats and ropes to beat the stallion in the face. He lashed his head back

/ 60 /

and forth, snapping like an enraged dog. One of the horses squealed as he was bitten. The men yelled and cursed.

Finally the Ghost was forced away from the fence. He retreated toward the center of the corral, and as he did, the loop tightened around his neck. He snorted and tossed his head, trying to shake it off. Mr. Claypool's rope settled on him from the other side.

Then the Ghost went crazy. He screamed, reared, kicked and hurled himself across the corral, scattering the mares and colts before him. The ropes stayed taut, as the horse and rider on each side maneuvered to hold the Ghost between them. The stallion's breathing turned ragged and labored. He buck-jumped to a halt, his front legs splayed out, his head down. He made a peculiar coughing sound, like a great bellows.

"He's choking!" Molly cried, but the men didn't slacken the ropes.

The Ghost swayed unsteadily, took a half-step forward and then crashed to the ground.

Three men ran into the corral, awkward in their high-heeled boots. One of them grabbed the Ghost's ear and twisted it. Another slipped a halter over his head. The third fastened hobbles onto the horse's front legs. They stripped the two ropes from his neck. The whole thing took just a few seconds. Then the men ran out again.

"*Wa-hooo!*" Vernon Claypool yelled and swung his hat. "Look at them go! I never saw three fellers move so fast in all my life. But you can bet I wouldn't want to be in the corral when that horse gets up, either."

The Ghost scrambled back to his feet. He took a few steps, stumbling in the hobbles that held his front legs. He tried to run, fell to his knees, and lurched awkwardly back to his feet. He half-reared, pawing at one leg with the other. Every time he tried to run, he tripped himself and nearly fell.

Molly felt sick. It was like seeing a noble king in chains, made clumsy and helpless.

"We'd better hobble the lead mare, too," Mr. Claypool said.

Once again, the ropes came out and the men closed in on the black mare. Molly watched. There wasn't anything else to do.

The next morning she was awakened by her father's voice outside the little tent where she slept with Alison.

"Rise and shine, sleepyheads. It's nearly daylight."

Alison groaned and pulled her sleeping bag over her head. Molly burrowed deeper, too, until she remembered that this was the day they would take the Ghost home. She sat up, running her fingers through her tousled hair. There didn't seem to be any more light coming through the tent now than there had been when she crawled in the night before.

She crept on hands and knees over to the door flap and peered through the zippered mosquito netting. There was a faint light of dawn, after all. She smelled woodsmoke from a campfire and heard the clinking of tin utensils as somebody prepared food. A distant bird made sleepy morning twitters. A horse whinnied and another one answered. Molly felt around for her jeans and boots.

"You've got my leg. Leave me alone," Alison mumbled grouchily. She woke up slowly and was always cross in the morning.

"Sorry." Molly slipped on her clothes and crawled outside, remembering to zip up the tent behind her. Mosquitos were quick to find ways to get in. She went immediately to the corral, her eyes searching until she found the dim shape of the Ghost. He'd been tied to one of the big junipers as extra insurance that he wouldn't get away. He turned his head to look at her and snorted in warning. She stopped.

"It may not be so bad," she told him. "You may get used to us and find out that people are okay. It'll be quieter when we get home and there's nobody around but you and me and Dad. Don't fight the ropes and hobbles and you won't get hurt."

If only he could understand. The girl watched him a moment more and then went to the fire. Dad handed her a hot drink made from powdered milk and cocoa. She took a sip and felt the warm liquid run down and spread out in her stomach. Les was sitting propped up nearby, drinking coffee.

"How do you feel?" she asked him.

"So-so." He didn't look well. His face was gray and tired as if he hadn't slept. A stubble of beard made him look older than his age, and his arrogant look was gone. Somehow she liked him better than she ever had before. Her feelings must have shown in her expression, because a little smile came into Les's eyes and one corner of his mouth turned up.

"I'll make it," he said.

It didn't take long until breakfast was over. All the camp equipment was loaded onto the pack animals. As Molly tightened her cinch, Alison came up behind her.

"I'm sorry I was crabby this morning," she said.

"That's okay. I'm used to it by now."

They grinned, understanding how well they knew each other.

Just as Molly got into the saddle, she saw the men taking down the opening to the corral. Except for the Ghost and the black lead mare who were hobbled, each of the wild horses had been snubbed up to either a ranch-raised horse or one of the men's saddle horns. The wild ones were white-eyed with panic, fighting the ropes, kicking up dust.

The Ghost bolted toward the hills, the black mare close behind him. They were slow and awkward in their hobbles and were easily turned back. They tried again and again to escape, and each time a rider was there, yelling, swinging a rope in their faces. The horses' hides grew shiny with sweat even in the cool morning air.

At last the men got them all lined out and headed in the right direction. The colts stayed close to their mothers' sides. The Ghost stumbled along, tripping over the unaccustomed restraints. His large dark eyes flashed defiantly, searching in all directions for a way out.

Molly rode at one side of the herd so that she could watch the stallion, even though she felt a pang every time she looked at him. She could see Les on the other side of the wild horses. Both hands rested on the saddle horn, and now and then he raised himself up a little, as though trying to find a position that didn't hurt so much.

Last night Dad had said that they were nearly twenty miles from home. It promised to be a long, tough ride.

/ 66 /

/ SEVEN /

Molly stood by the small corral, looking at the Ghost inside. Dad had put another row of poles on top, just in case the horse thought about trying to jump out. They'd arrived home the day before and kept the Ghost snubbed up to the center post ever since. They'd given him food and water, but he'd refused the hay and knocked over the pail.

"What are we going to do with you?" Molly murmured.

Just then a car came up the lane carrying Alison and her family. Molly went to meet them. Dad had invited the neighbors to a chili supper, and the Edwardses had come early to help her fix it.

Alison's mother brought several loaves of home-baked bread and some pies. Molly had put beans to soak the night before and baked two pans of brownies that morning. She and Mrs. Edwards now cut chuck roast into cubes, browned it, and started it simmering in two big kettles. Alison began making salad.

"This is going to be a good supper," Molly said.

Mrs. Edwards smiled. "I think so. Those brownies look delicious. You're so capable, Molly." She looked at her appraisingly. "And growing like a weed, just like Alison. I'm going to take her shopping soon. You come with us, and we'll get you some new jeans. Those are getting a little short."

Molly looked at her ankles. "I guess they are. I hadn't noticed." Dad hadn't, either. He didn't pay much attention to clothes, although every once in awhile he'd say, "Why don't you look through the catalog and see if there's anything you want." But most of the time they both forgot. It was usually Mrs. Edwards or Mrs. Claypool who suggested to Molly that maybe she needed something new.

If her mother had lived, they would have looked through the catalog together, picking out things for her to wear to school. Or they'd have gone to town together, shop in the morning and see a movie in the afternoon. Or maybe they'd have picked out patterns and fabrics to sew together, one thing for Molly and one for Mother. Her heart ached for all the things she'd missed.

As if she'd read her mind, Mrs. Edwards spoke. "Molly, you look more like your father every day. Except for your eyes, of course. They're dark like your mother's, and so often you have the same kind of expression."

Molly thought of the sober dark eyes in the old pictures, eyes that always looked straight into the camera. Did she really look that serious? She was glad to hear that otherwise she took after her father. She thought him very good-looking with his lean brown face and feathery dark hair.

A pickup truck drove in. More neighbors had arrived. They all went out to the corral to look at the Ghost before they even came in the house. He hated it, Molly knew—all those dreadful two-legged creatures pointing at him, talking at him through the bars; and there was no way for him to escape to the quiet of the hills.

She heard the sound of thumping and then a burst of yells. She went out onto the porch. Someone had released the rope that held the Ghost's head close to the pole and he was loose in the corral. He galloped around the small interior, head high, looking for a way out.

Her great-uncle, August Parker, stepped out on the porch with her.

"Do you think the Ghost will get away?" she

asked hopefully. "Maybe he'll break out of the corral."

Uncle August shook his gray head. "Not a chance. Not that corral. Your dad built it strong enough to hold the range bulls when he brings them in. It'll sure hold a horse."

The house filled up with people. Miss Miller came with the Claypools. She wore a pair of jeans about one size too small and a silky white shirt with a fringed yoke front and back. Every man in the room kept looking at her, including Les, who hopped around on crutches with his leg in a cast from ankle to thigh. Molly was glad to see that Dad appeared to notice Miss Miller, too. They spent quite a bit of time talking quietly in one corner of the living room. Les watched them, looking unhappy and curling up his lip.

Molly was disappointed when Uncle August went to join the two of them, and decided she might as well go over, too. She didn't suppose they'd say anything romantic with Dad's uncle standing there.

"I think it's so exciting that you were able to catch the Ghost when no one else could do it," Miss Miller said as Molly came within hearing distance. "I heard stories about him when I first came here. I understand that dozens of men tried to catch him for years and years, but you're the only one who ever did."

"I had a lot of help," Jim Parker said modestly.

"I'm sorry I wasn't able to go along, but I'm mighty glad to be rid of a prime source of trouble," Uncle August said.

"I suppose you mean that the Ghost is a trouble-maker because he steals mares. Is that it?" asked Miss Miller.

"That's part of it," Uncle August said. "But all wild horses are troublemakers. Forage is scarce in this country, anyhow, and they eat grass that should go to the cattle that bring in cash to the ranchers. What the broncs don't eat, they tear up and trample into the ground. I'd be happy if we could get rid of all the wild horses. They're just pests, no good at all."

"Oh, how can you say that?" Miss Miller sounded shocked. "They're so beautiful. The Ghost is really magnificent."

"Yeah, the Ghost is a beautiful horse," Uncle August agreed grudgingly. "There's good blood in his veins—Arab, maybe. Probably his granddam or grandsire was a feral horse, one that belonged to somebody and then got loose and went wild. The Ghost isn't scruffy enough to be a real wild horse."

"I'm surprised to hear you call a wild horse scruffy. I thought cowboys loved horses."

Uncle August chuckled. "We may love horses, but the wild ones are broom tails, jug heads, and that's

different. They're not pretty horses. Folks like you, from back east, have a different view of wild horses than folks that live out here right with them. They breed so fast that they get to be varmints, like prairie dogs or coyotes. Used to be that ranchers would join together and hire a man to go out and shoot a few, just to thin the herds."

"Jim, do you agree with this?" Miss Miller turned to Molly's father.

"Well, it is true that the average wild horse looks a lot more romantic at a distance than close-up. I'd hate to shoot one of them, though."

"It's absolutely cruel to shoot a wild horse. I'm surprised that men who work with horses as much as you people do could be so heartless. Don't you think wild animals have a right to live? Isn't there a measure other than just profit?"

Molly could tell by the tight look around Uncle August's mouth that he was starting to get angry. She'd heard the neighbors talk about wild horses all of her life and knew that sometimes they were a problem. Just the same, she agreed with her teacher that shooting them was a pretty rotten thing to do. She didn't want Miss Miller and Uncle August to get into an argument over wild horses, though, so she took him by the arm.

"Uncle August, I need you to come taste the chili

for me. I'm not sure I've got enough chili powder in it and you can always tell when it's right."

Dad winked at her as she led the older man away to the kitchen.

Everyone ate as much as they could hold and then sat around in the big living room. By now Uncle August was in a good mood again.

"Say, Les, I hear you broke your leg chasing a wild horse."

"Yep. The horse got away, too."

"Tough luck." Uncle August shook his head in sympathy.

"Les is pretty gritty," said Dad. "He walked more than a mile on that broken leg, with two cracked ribs and packing his saddle."

"I paid a lot of money for that saddle," Les said. "It was hand carved by Joe Pounds. I wasn't about to leave it."

"That was quite a walk in your condition," Uncle August went on. "Must have hurt some."

Les looked directly into Molly's eyes as he replied, "Not much." If she hadn't seen how pale and sweaty he was when she found him, she couldn't have been sure that he was lying. She smiled at him and he winked. Maybe he did look sulky and act proud as a rooster sometimes, but he was tough.

"Do you remember Karl Remmy?" Mr. Edwards asked. "He worked for me for a couple of years. He hit his thumb with a hammer once while we were patching the barn. It didn't seem too bad at the time, but it kept swelling up as the day went on. By midnight it had swelled so much under the nail that he just couldn't stand it anymore He said that it throbbed as if it had been hit with a hammer all over again every time his heart beat.

"Well, it's more than fifty miles to the nearest doctor from my place. So Karl took a hand drill, held the handle in his teeth and cranked away with his right hand. He proceeded to drill on his left thumbnail. Now and then he splashed a little whiskey on it to numb it. Could be he himself took a drink now and then as an anesthetic. Pretty soon he'd drilled a hole in the nail, enough to relieve the pressure and the worst of the pain."

"A fellow can do most anything, if he really has to," Uncle August said. "I heard of a man who lived in a cabin up on Clear Creek, about thirty years ago. He got snowed in. During that time he got such a bad toothache that he gouged his tooth out with a jackknife and a pair of pliers. Now, I don't know if that's a true story or not, but it might be. A really bad toothache, one that lasted for days, might drive a man near crazy."

Their voices rose and fell, recounting stories of other people, other times. Molly and Alison lay on the floor, listening. After awhile, somebody said, "Did you bring your fiddle, Uncle August?" Everybody called him Uncle August, but he was blood uncle to Molly's father. He got out his fiddle and Dad picked up his harmonica. The music began with "Strawberry Roan."

Later, Molly rose quietly and went outside. The music followed her, a sad song this time. Uncle August's fiddle wailed a long high note. A coyote close by must have heard it, for it raised its voice in a keening cry. Another answered and they yammered together, somewhere out in the dark toward the cliffs of the Palisades.

In the bright starlight, Molly could dimly see the small corral. Inside, the pale, wraithlike shape that was the Ghost circled around and around within its bars.

/ EIGHT /

When Molly went out in the morning, the Ghost stood quietly in the middle of the corral. Maybe he would settle in; maybe he'd learn not to mind fences, the girl thought. Just then he saw her and threw up his head with a snort. He lunged into the poles. Molly retreated quickly, but the horse smashed against the bars again and again until a trickle of blood ran down his chest. The ranch horses moved uneasily in their big corral when they heard the commotion.

Molly's father came up beside her.

"Let's turn him loose," she said. "He'll never be happy here."

"We can't do that. He'll just keep on stealing mares, from here or from some other ranch."

"We could take him way out into the badlands,

some place so far that he could never find the trail back."

"No, kid, it wouldn't work. If we could find our way back, so could he." Dad sighed. "Now that I've got him, I don't know what to do with him."

"Maybe it will be all right." Molly spoke the meaningless words to make him feel better. But maybe it *would* be all right. Maybe she could make it that way. The Ghost had come to her twice out of the wild. He must understand how she felt about him. If she tried, really hard, then maybe, just maybe . . .

She rushed through her chores. As soon as she finished, she went outside with a book from the county library. When the stallion showed signs of uneasiness, indicating that she was close enough, she sat on the ground. She opened the book and began to read. Once in awhile, she looked at him to see what he was doing. He was watching her. She read sitting up until she felt her back would crack; then she lay on her stomach and read some more. After a couple of hours, she eased to her feet and went into the house.

She continued doing that as often as she could take time from her work around the house. In three days, Molly could walk right up to the corral. The Ghost backed edgily away, as far as he could get from her, but he no longer tried to smash his way out

when she came close. Her father was a different matter. However softly Dad spoke or however carefully he moved, the stallion flew into a frenzy whenever any man came near.

Dad put a small wooden water trough in the corral for the horse, but they never saw him drink. They gave him hay and grain, but the Ghost trampled both into the dust as he circled restlessly, endlessly about the inside of his prison. His eyes looked out past the ranch buildings, toward the Palisades and the hills beyond the river.

Mr. Claypool came over one afternoon. He regarded the horse who glared back at him. The man took an easy step forward and the stallion whirled so fast that he crashed sideway into the bars. He slipped down on one knee, and when he scrambled to his feet again, there were red marks on the side of his head where he'd scraped off the skin.

"What are you going to do with him, Jim? You can't break an animal like that, not the age he is and him being wild all his life."

"He's a fine-looking horse, nothing like the average broom tail," Dad said, not really answering the question.

"Yeah. He's mighty fine-looking, a real pretty horse. But he don't look so good now."

It was true. His moon-colored coat was dark with

dried sweat, dust, and caked blood. His ribs were starting to show.

"Has he been eating anything?" Mr. Claypool asked.

Dad shook his head. "Very little, if anything, but he drinks water, probably at night when no one's around."

"If he won't eat—and wild animals sometimes won't—he'll starve himself to death. It might be better to put him down right now. At least it'll be quick."

Put him down. The words fell like lead on Molly. She knew what they meant. The Ghost would be shot. If she was going to save his life, she'd have to try harder to gentle him before it was too late.

She took an apple to the corral. The Ghost had probably never tasted one, but maybe the smell would tempt him. Slowly, timidly, Molly moved up to the bars. The horse backed away, ears laid back tight to his head so he looked mean and ugly. She rolled the apple gently across the ground. He whirled and slammed into the fence as the apple was split into pieces beneath his trampling hoofs.

Angry words erupted from Molly before she could stop them. "You stupid horse!" she yelled. "Why are you so stubborn? I'm trying to save your life. Why can't you be like other horses?"

She waved her arm toward the pasture where Cappy and Solita grazed contentedly. Cappy raised his head and looked toward them as he heard the sound of her voice. The Ghost flinched and tossed his head. His haunches bumped against the corral as he tried to back farther away.

Molly gritted her teeth so hard that her jaws ached. She wanted to scream and howl in frustration, to beat on the ground, to beat on the Ghost. He was so stubborn, so infuriating, so impossible.

She rushed to the barn. She grabbed a halter off the wall and hurried across the pasture. Cappy came to meet her, and she slipped the halter over his head. As soon as she got him through the gate, she grabbed his mane and swung up on him bareback. She booted him in the ribs and he broke into a lope, then a run. They raced away from the ranch and up the trail to the Point of the Palisades. Cappy slowed before they reached the top. His sides heaved and he felt warm against Molly's thighs, but he trotted perkily along, ready to run some more if that was what she wanted. Instead, she guided him over to the edge of the cliff so she could look off into the country beyond.

The girl sat there a long time, gazing across the sheer drop to the river below, out into the land where the Ghost had lived. It looked hazy and golden in the morning sunlight, but Molly knew it was harsh and unforgiving. It took a special kind of horse to find the scarce grass and water, to survive the heat of summer and the desolation of winter. Only a certain kind of horse—tough, wary, and stubborn—could have avoided the men who had hunted him for so long. If the Ghost were like other horses, docile and trainable, then he wouldn't be the Ghost at all, but just an ordinary horse. Her rage and frustration ebbed away, drawn out by the vast regions before her.

When she returned to the ranch and saw the Ghost again, she was saddened by his ribbed sides and dispirited eyes. She dismounted, unfastened the corral gate but didn't open it. The horse was literally dying to go home, homesick to the point of death. It was in her power to set him free. All she had to do was open the gate and step back. Then he would run and run forever, away from the ranch, past the Palisades, and back across the river.

And when Dad came home, what would he say? How would he feel? He'd brought in the Ghost when no one else had been able to do it. He'd gone after him because the stallion had taken his favorite horse, Solita. How long would it be until the Ghost came back after the mare? It wasn't fair to sneak behind Dad's back.

She fastened the gate again, feeling a hard lump of despair in the pit of her stomach, as if she'd dropped a hanging noose over the Ghost's neck.

"Damn!" she said in a loud voice.

"That's a word for grown-ups, Molly." She heard her father's voice and saw him a few yards away. He'd said the same thing to her years ago, the first time she'd ever tried any swear words. "And that was a grown-up decision you made, to fasten the gate."

"But I want to open it again, real quick."

"No, it was too much work and expense to get him once. But it's plain we can't keep him. I hate to say it, but I think we'd better end the whole thing right now."

"No! We haven't had him very long. Maybe he'll settle in. I'll keep trying, and maybe he'll get used to us. Just look how beautiful he is. You can't just shoot him, as if he were something mean and worthless."

Dad rubbed the back of his neck as if it hurt him. "I know you hope some sort of miracle will occur, and I do, too. But it won't. You are right about one thing, though. I can't just shoot him—I don't want to be the one to put an end to a legend. But I can't turn him loose, either. I wish to God I'd never caught him."

* * *

Jim Parker was busy moving the cattle to the summer range, and he was rarely around the house during the day. Instead of going with him, as she normally would, Molly doubled the time spent near the corral. She picked fresh grass and dropped little piles through the bars. Although the blades dried in the sun apparently untouched, it seemed the horse was becoming more used to her. He'd been in the corral for a week now. He didn't watch her every minute as he had before. Sometimes she would look up from her book or her mending to see the Ghost not looking in her direction at all but staring off toward the south. She could circle the corral on the outside, and while he kept turning so that he always faced her, the horse was no longer so fearful.

If I could just touch you, the girl thought. *If you would only learn that I don't want to hurt you, that being touched can be okay, then maybe . . .*

Sometimes Molly imagined herself stroking and petting the Ghost, softly, gently, until he learned to like it. When he was accustomed to being touched, she would coax him over to the fence so she could slip one leg over his back. She wouldn't jump on all at once, but would gradually let him get used to the idea and the feel of her weight on him. Pretty soon he would stand quietly and let her sit on his back. Soon he would be enough at ease so that he would walk around the corral carrying her. Then she would call Dad and show him how she had gentled the Ghost.

After awhile she would be able to ride him anywhere, bareback and with only a hackamore, so he would never have to feel the iron bit in his mouth. He would prance along in his springy trot, feet high, neck arched, silvery tail plumed out. People would point at them and say, "That's Molly Parker. She's the girl who tamed the Ghost."

Molly roused herself from her daydream and looked at the white stallion. His head drooped until his nose nearly touched the ground. His ribs showed through his dull, scruffy coat. His half-closed eyes were lackluster. He looked sick, no longer the splendid creature who had appeared like a vision to her in the past. She saw by the way Dad studied the horse in the evening that he was aware of the deterioration.

"He's getting used to me," she assured him. "I saw him nosing some grass today. He may have eaten a little." The last was a lie, but maybe tomorrow he would really do it.

Her father didn't play music in the evenings anymore or dance with Molly in the kitchen. Instead he sat at his desk, doing accounts and writing checks with a frown on his face.

"There's a dance at the Grange Hall tonight. Do you want to go?" he asked her on Saturday. He didn't sound interested, only polite.

"No, you go if you want."

"Might be good for you to get out. You haven't been off the place in over a week."

"I don't want to go." Her head ached. She couldn't bear the thought of having to talk to anyone, of having to smile and be nice and answer questions about the Ghost.

Dad stayed home, too, slouched in a chair all evening, reading a book from the library. Molly sat on the porch awhile, but it was a chilly night. The sky was overcast, clouds hiding the moon and stars, as if summer had passed and winter were already here.

She thought of the Grange Hall, which would be bright, noisy, and crowded with people. Maybe Miss Miller would be there. Molly had been so absorbed in thoughts of the Ghost that she'd forgotten all about her. She should have said she wanted to go to the dance, and then Dad would have gone, too. Right now Uncle August would be up on the little stage with the rest of the band. He'd smile, stomp his foot, and play up a storm on his fiddle. The dancers down on the floor would skip, weave and shuffle through the intricate square dance steps, while the caller half-chanted, half-sang:

"Chicken in the bread pan, kickin' out dough.
Grab your partner and do-si-do."

The music and the dancers seemed a thousand long, dark miles away from Molly.

* * *

It rained the next day, a steady gray drizzle. It was too wet to go outside. Molly saw the Ghost standing dejectedly in the corral, his coat darkened and dripping with water. Everything in the house seemed damp and clammy.

Alison called in the middle of the afternoon. "You should have come to the dance. We had a good time. Several of the kids from school were there. Larry asked about you. Do you still think he's cute?"

"Sort of," she said, but without really caring. She could barely remember what he looked like. She felt indifferent to Alison, too, even though the girl was her best friend and had been for her entire life.

Alison's voice barely reached her. It was frail and tinny. There were other sounds on the line, like wind. Molly imagined all the distances the thin phone line traveled, across the miles that separated her from her friend. It stretched over sagebrush, hills and stony creek beds, carrying their words. She imagined the words sliding along the wire like clinging beads of moisture, changing shape as they slipped along, nearly blown off by the wind.

"Miss Miller was there," Alison went on.

"Oh, was she?"

"She came with Les." The line crackled and hissed. "Les couldn't dance because of his leg, but she sat with him all evening. They held hands." The wind sounds thrummed along the wire, and Alison's voice faded away, blown off the line at last.

"I can't hear you, Alison. You'll have to talk louder."

"I have to tell you the rest," she shouted in Molly's ear. "I saw them kissing out in the hall. Les told my dad they might get married."

"Oh. Well. Thanks for telling me."

"I'm really sorry, Molly."

"Yeah, I am, too. There's something the matter with the phone. I have to hang up. I'll talk to you later."

Just before she put down the phone, Molly heard a long desolate howl on the line, like the voice of coming winter.

/ NINE /

S unday dawned clear and bright without a hint of a cloud in the sky. The radio was on playing church music, and Dad had cooked oatmeal with brown sugar and a handful of raisins plumped up in it.

"I've saddled the horses. We'll take a ride after breakfast."

They went out to the horses, and she gathered up Cappy's reins.

"You go on down to the ford," her father said. "I thought of something I have to do. I'll catch you in a minute."

His voice had a strained, unnatural sound, and she glanced at him. His back was turned and he fiddled with his cinch. It seemed to take him a long time to adjust it.

"Go on," he said impatiently.

"I know why you want me to go ahead. You've decided to shoot the Ghost, haven't you?"

"You know we can't keep him, Molly. There isn't a fence built that will hold him. It isn't right to keep him in that little corral, penned up and miserable, until he starves himself to death. You go to the river, and I'll get it over with." His voice was harsh. He went to the house to get his rifle.

The oatmeal Molly had eaten for breakfast threatened to rise up into her throat. She swallowed several times. She scuffed toward the corral, and Cappy followed her. The Ghost watched indifferently, his once fine eyes dull with despair. Molly slumped forward and rested her chin on a pole.

"Oh, Ghost, I'm sorry. It shouldn't end this way."

In her mind's eye rose the memory of the way he'd looked the first time she ever saw him, on a summer day back in a time when everything seemed perfect. Dimly she heard her mother laughing and her own high childish giggles. Then both of them were hushed into silence as the Ghost came down to the water's edge to watch the human creatures at their play. He floated across the river, a mystical magical steed from a fairy tale. Drops of water sparkled beneath him, shimmering in the sunlight.

Water dimmed Molly's vision and it almost seemed that she was still back in that other time. But these were tears, distorting the image of the Ghost who was before her, standing against the poles on the opposite side of the corral. She reached into her pocket for a handkerchief, and her fingers fumbled over little hard squares. Sugar cubes. She'd tried to tempt the stallion with them once.

I'll try one more time, she thought.

The Ghost watched her come. He didn't move as she inched closer and closer along the outside of the poles. She was so close that she could see the whiskers on his chin, a fly crawling on the tangled white mane, the pink insides of his ears. Slowly, slowly, she stretched out her hand with a sugar cube on it.

The inside of the corral seemed to explode. Hoofs flashed high in the air and drummed on the bars like thunder. Dust rose in spurts. The Ghost's eyes lit with the force of a proud and terrible spirit. He screamed, a wild piercing cry. He hurled himself at the opposite side of the corral and seemed to climb up the bars like a huge cat. The top pole cracked and the horse fell back. He scrambled to his feet and galloped around the corral. Twice he flashed in front of Molly, his powerful body just a few feet away.

The Ghost launched himself in a desperate leap. The highest bar splintered and fell to the ground as the horse went over the top. His head and tail lifted. Like a cloud scudding before the wind, he fled to-

ward the Palisades and the badlands beyond.

Molly jumped on Cappy and then heard her father yelling behind her. She didn't know what she was going to do, but she had to follow the Ghost. Cappy stretched out in a dead run. She leaned low over his neck. His mane lashed against her face as, for the second time, she raced in pursuit of the wild stallion.

As they neared the river, Molly saw Vernon Claypool and another man riding up the trail. The man had been hired temporarily to take Les's place until his leg healed. The Ghost saw them, too, and he took the turn to the Point. The men whooped and rushed in pursuit.

There was only one trail and it ended at the Point. The Ghost had trapped himself. When Molly and Cappy reached the top, she saw the stallion run up to the rim. He skidded to a stop and looked at the river far below. He whirled and raced back toward the riders.

Dad had caught up with them. He raised his rifle and took aim between the Ghost's eyes as the horse charged at him. Molly swerved Cappy so that he ran into Solita. The rifle barrel was jolted up and the bullet shot off into the sky. She had a brief glimpse of her father's startled eyes just before the two horses separated. The Ghost leaped away at the sound of the shot. Mr. Claypool and the hired man closed in. The man lifted his rope and shook out a loop. The Ghost galloped back toward the rim.

He didn't even slow down as he neared the edge, but raced on full stride. He leaped off the Point of the Palisades, so wide and far that it seemed he would sail clear over the river and out into the badlands on the other side. No living horse could ever leap that far. Only a phantom could, traveling through the air with supernatural power.

The Ghost fluttered against the sky, mane and tail like pennants of silver. It appeared that he would float through the air like thistledown and land safely on the other side. Then suddenly he plunged out of sight below the edge of the cliff.

Molly peered over the rim. The Ghost's head came up out of the swirling water just above the rapids. She saw his white forelegs flailing, then he was whirled away in the long, plunging chute through the canyon. She caught one glimpse of his pale head among the rocks and the white-capped water. She didn't see him again.

In the sudden stillness, the only sound was the blowing of the horses. The four people sat without speaking, their eyes on the river. Dad shifted in the saddle and the leather creaked.

"No horse could survive that jump and the rapids,

too. But I'll go down and look a little just the same."
Dad's voice was subdued.

They found no tracks coming out of the water and
no sign of the Ghost. The rushing water could carry
a body for miles or wedge it between rocks where it
would be almost impossible to find. Molly and her father parted from Mr. Claypool and his hired man.
The Parkers rode home without speaking.

"Some creatures are born to live free," Dad said at
last. "A death in freedom is better than one in captivity."

Once again, her father had the horses saddled
when Molly came down for breakfast the next morning.

"Let's take a ride," he said.

"Why?"

"I just feel like it."

Jim Parker was sober and quiet as they jogged to
the river. Molly thought she knew why. They had
hardly spoken to each other since they'd returned
from Palisades Point the day before. Molly's heart
had been heavy, and she'd been filled with conflict-
ing emotions. So many thoughts and words jammed
up together in her mind that it seemed as if none of
them could get out. She hadn't known how her father felt. In fact, she'd been so preoccupied with her-

self that she hadn't given much thought to him.

"Dad, I don't blame you for what happened to the Ghost," she said now, wanting to clear the air which seemed to hang close and thick around them. "I understand why you wanted to catch him. You couldn't just let Solita go and not do anything to get her back. If Cappy had been run off somehow, I'd want him back, too."

"You're remarkably understanding, Molly. But then you've always been more grown-up than some people ever get. When you were just a little tot, your mother used to say that you were four going on thirty-five."

They rode in silence for awhile and then he went on. "I always hated the thought of shooting the Ghost, but there were times when it seemed the only way out. I thought about turning him loose again, but just couldn't do it. It's crazy how a man gets so stubborn sometimes, so dead set on only one way of doing things. That beautiful horse going off the cliff was a sad ending, but maybe it was the only possible ending. There don't seem many other reasonable alternatives."

Maybe it isn't ended, Molly thought. She couldn't say the words out loud, because her throat swelled up and her eyes prickled so that she knew she'd cry if she tried to speak. But her mother had been gone for six years, and yet she still lived on in the thoughts of Molly and her father. Her mother always would live in memory. And now the Ghost was there, too. Both her mother and the wild stallion would live for as long as Molly herself lived. Sometime she'd tell her father that, when she felt stronger, but right now her feelings were too new and raw to speak aloud.

They reached the river, crossed at the ford, and went down below the rapids on the other side. Dad got off his horse and she did, too. He didn't explain, but she knew they were looking for tracks. Hours passed with little speech between them except for comments now and then on animal tracks, a cactus in brief splendid bloom, a rattle of rocks as something hurried through the brush away from them. They ate a light lunch that Molly's father had packed in his saddlebag.

"I hear Les and the school teacher are going steady," he said.

"Yes, Alison told me. I'm sorry it turned out that way, Dad."

"Don't be sorry on my account. It was you that had her picked out, not me. It may seem strange to you, but I don't want to get married again. Your mother was so special to me, and we were so close to each other that it was enough to last me for the rest of my life. I don't want to settle for anything only half as good.

"But I do understand that it's hard for you to be alone so much and that you've missed out on a lot because you don't have a mother. So I've talked to Alison's folks, and they'd be happy to have you live with them. You'll have a lot of company with Alison and her mom both there all the time. You won't have to work so hard, either. You can come home on weekends, if you want, and . . ."

She didn't hear the rest of what he said. She just saw her father coming home to an empty house and cooking his own supper, listening to the radio to all those sad night songs that can break a person's heart, playing the harmonica with no one to hear his music.

"I don't want to live with the Edwardses. It's nice of you to think of it, but I'd rather stay home."

"Don't make up your mind too quick."

"Maybe I'll spend the night more often with Alison, and she can stay more at our place. But I'd rather be home with you. Sure, I get lonely sometimes, but I might be lonely at Alison's, too, because I'd always be just living there, not really part of their family. We'll get along fine, just as we are. Don't we always get along just fine?"

"Yeah, we do. We get along just fine." Dad took her hand for a moment and then began to put away the lunch things.

"You know," Molly said thoughtfuly. "If Miss

Miller could love Les, she sure wouldn't be right for you."

"Les is all right. He's just young, the same as she is."

"I suppose so."

They started toward home, and after awhile, he started to whistle. Molly realized that she hadn't heard him whistle for a long time, since before the Ghost was captured. Her heart lifted, lightening with the sound of the music. She was so glad that he was her father. She knew the words and she sang softly along.

> *"Hush, little baby, don't say a word.*
> *Daddy's gonna buy you a mockingbird.*
> *And if that mockingbird don't sing,*
> *Daddy's gonna buy you a diamond ring."*

As they reached a pool below the rapids, she saw a cleft back in a shadowy curve of the rocks. "Dad, look at that. Have you ever noticed it before?"

"Not especially. Let's see how far back it goes."

Cappy and Solita waded through shallow water to reach the narrow opening, like a door left slightly ajar. They entered the passage, barely wide enough for a horse to pass single file. They climbed steeply and soon came out behind some scrubby trees up on a rocky ledge. The badlands spread below, fierce and barren in the hot light of the sun.

Molly saw something white hanging from a branch on one of the trees. She picked off several long silvery hairs from a horse's mane or tail. She showed them to Dad.

"Could they be from the Ghost?"

"They might be. I believe almost anything is possible, Molly."

She knew that there were other white horses, or that the stallion could have lost the hairs another time if he had climbed up to the ledge. The rocks showed no tracks, no sign. Molly and her father looked out at the badlands, as empty and alien as the face of the moon. Nothing moved out there, not even a buzzard.

Whole herds could vanish without a trace in that vast empty country. Just because they didn't see him didn't mean he wasn't there.

Molly looped the silver hair into a ring around her finger and put it in her pocket. She looked once more at the wild mysterious country before they started home. Her heart ached with the longing that her wish was true.

Be out there somewhere, Ghost. Be out there forever.